The *...erman*

Illustrated by ...
Cover Illustration by ...

AWARD ... ITED

John was down by the seashore with his cousin Ella. He had been busy building sandcastles, when suddenly he noticed that Ella was crying.

"What's the matter, Ella?" he asked, throwing down his spade, and running over to her.

"I have lost my lovely ring," she sobbed.

"Where did you lose it?" asked John. "Let's go and hunt for it. I'm sure it won't take long to find."

"It's no use," said Ella, drying her eyes. "I lost it when I was out in the boat this morning. It fell off my finger as I was trailing my hand in the water, and before I could do anything, I saw it sinking down to the bottom of the sea."

"If only I knew the way there, I'd go and hunt for your ring," said John. "But I would drown if I went deep into the water."

"Of course you would, silly," said Ella, smiling. "Carry on building castles, and forget about my ring!"

John went off and thought hard as he dug in the sand.

"I'm sure I'd find that ring, if I could find someone to guide me under the sea," he said to himself.

"Well, I'll take you if you like!" said a sweet voice near him. John looked up in surprise. He saw a fairy sitting on a rock, with long hair blowing in the wind.

"I've never seen a fairy before!" he cried in delight. "Are you really a fairy?"

"Yes, really," she answered. "I'm on my way to visit my sister Pinkity, who married a merman. I heard what you said, as I was flying by, and I wondered if you'd like to come with me."

"Oh I *would*!" cried John. "Do please take me."

"Come along then," said the fairy,

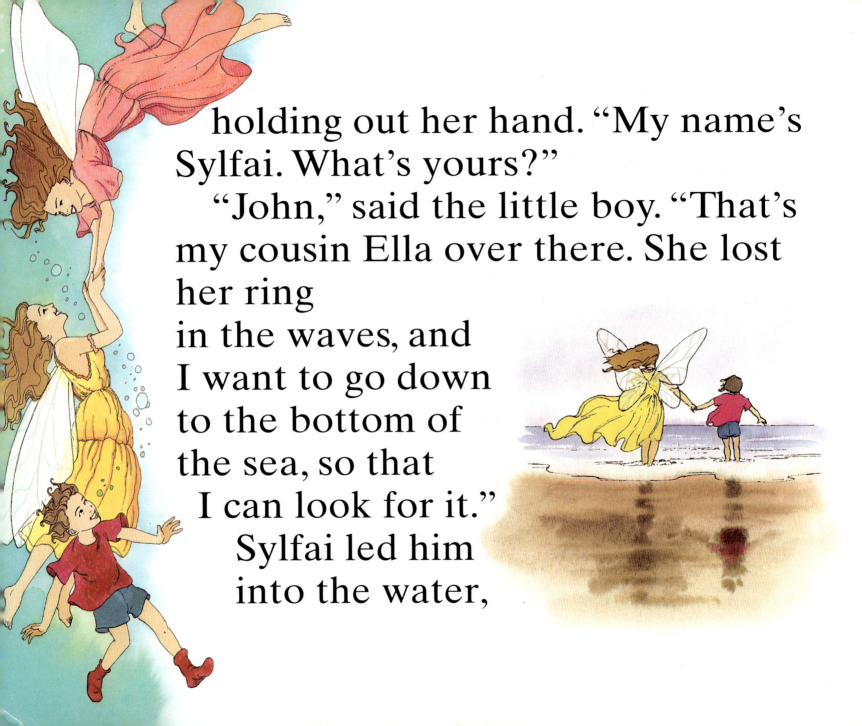

holding out her hand. "My name's Sylfai. What's yours?"

"John," said the little boy. "That's my cousin Ella over there. She lost her ring in the waves, and I want to go down to the bottom of the sea, so that I can look for it."

Sylfai led him into the water,

and it splashed over his socks. "Oh, dear, I'll get wet!" he said. "I won't drown, will I?"

"Oh, I forgot," said Sylfai. "I must rub you with a sea-spell, so that you can walk beneath the water safe and dry. What a good thing you reminded me!"

She put her hands in the water, and then made an outline around John's body, singing strange magic words as she did so.

"There! Now you'll be all right!" she said. "Come along."

They ran into the water, deeper and deeper, until John was right up to his waist. It wasn't at all difficult to walk in the sea, like it usually is. Soon he was up to his shoulders, and then suddenly his head went right under! But he didn't splutter or choke. It was just as easy breathing in the water as on the land. John thought it was really

wonderful. Bright fish swam
all around them, and beautiful
seaweed floated
everywhere.
   "We've a long
way to go, so we'll
find a fish to ride
on," said Sylfai.

She beckoned to a
big codfish, and soon she and
John were sitting comfortably on its
back, racing through the water.
Swish! Swish!

"I'm a little tired now," said the codfish at last. "Look, there's a crowd of jellyfish! Catch hold of the ribbons that hang down from them, and they'll carry you as far as you want to go!"

"Take us to Pinkity, the Silver Merman's wife!" cried Sylfai. The jellyfish moved off quickly, and soon they arrived at a lovely cave, where a fairy sat combing out her long hair.

Sylfai let go of the jellyfish, and ran to kiss her little sister. John followed her, feeling rather shy.

"Oh, Sylfai, how lovely to see you!" cried Pinkity. "And who is this with you?"

"This is John," said Sylfai. "He's come to look for a lovely ring that his cousin has lost in the sea."

"But the sea is such a big place – it would take him all his life to find it!" cried Pinkity. "Never mind, John, maybe you could take her a pretty piece of coral instead."

"Where's your husband?" asked Sylfai.

"Oh, he's gone to the Ocean Market," said Pinkity. "He'll be back soon, in time for tea."

She set a cloth on a rock, and put a jug of pretty seaweed in the middle. Then she put shells for plates, and cups made of pink coral. John couldn't think how anyone could drink out of a cup when there was water all around, but Sylfai said it was quite easy when you knew how! John was looking forward to trying.

Soon the meal was ready, and they took their places at the table. There was seaweed soup, pink and green jelly made from sea anemones, and starfish cakes. John was very hungry and, though he had never had such a strange meal before, he enjoyed it very much.

"Here's my husband!" cried Pinkity.
John looked up, and saw a fine big
merman swimming through the water.
He had a tail like a fish, and gleamed
like silver as he swam into the cave.

"Why, here's quite a party!" he
chuckled. "Who's our guest?"

"I'm John," said John. "I'm very pleased to meet you."

"Same to you," said the merman, and he sat down at the table, and helped himself to some jelly. He was very friendly, and he told John such funny stories about the fish

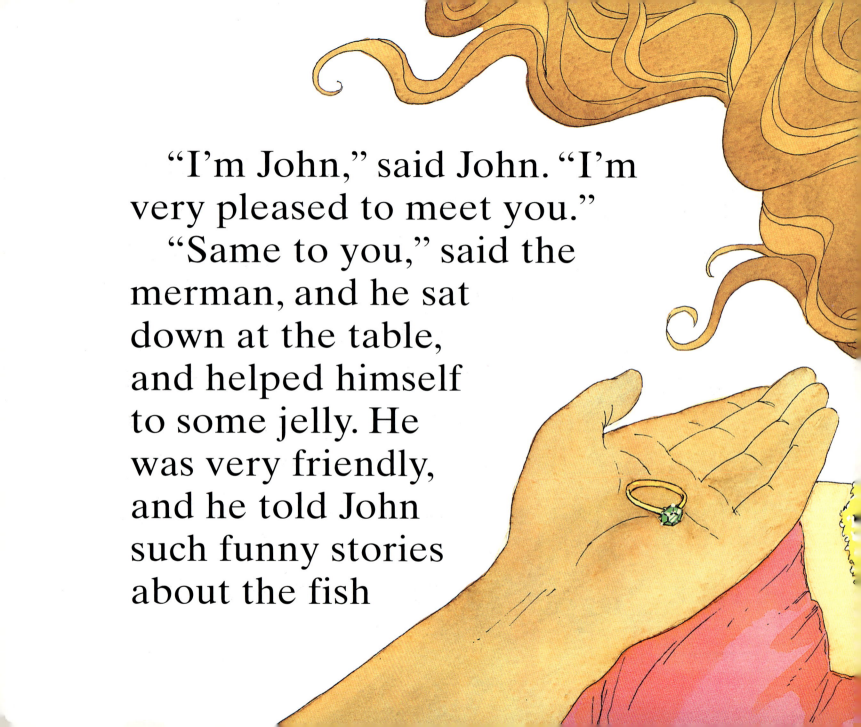

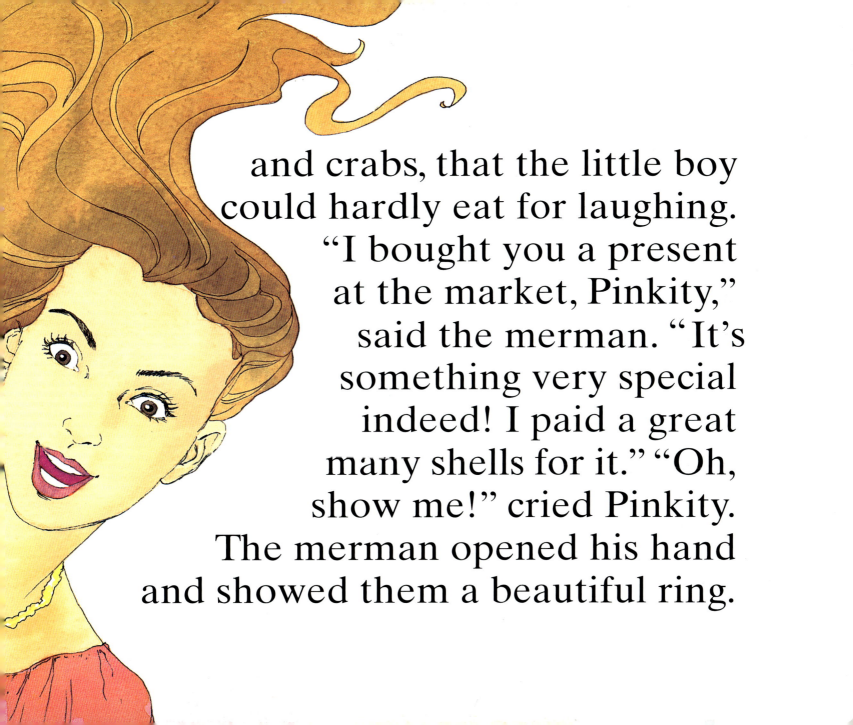

and crabs, that the little boy could hardly eat for laughing. "I bought you a present at the market, Pinkity," said the merman. "It's something very special indeed! I paid a great many shells for it." "Oh, show me!" cried Pinkity. The merman opened his hand and showed them a beautiful ring.

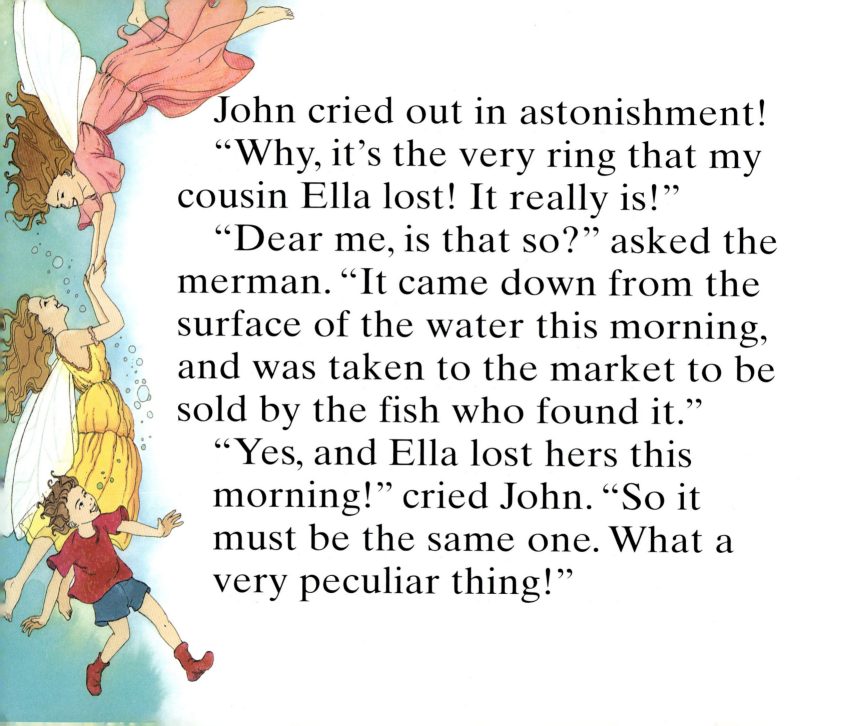

John cried out in astonishment! "Why, it's the very ring that my cousin Ella lost! It really is!"

"Dear me, is that so?" asked the merman. "It came down from the surface of the water this morning, and was taken to the market to be sold by the fish who found it."

"Yes, and Ella lost hers this morning!" cried John. "So it must be the same one. What a very peculiar thing!"

"Well, you must take it back to Ella," said Pinkity. "I couldn't keep it now I know that."

"Oh, no," said John, "your husband bought it, and he must give it to you. I'll tell Ella, and I'm sure she'll be pleased when she knows you have got it."

"No, you must take it," said the merman.

But John wouldn't, no matter how they begged him to. He was

quite sure Ella would rather
Pinkity had it.

"I really ought to go back now,"
he said. "Ella will be worried."

"I'll take you to the shore on
one of my white horses!" said
the merman. "They go very
fast indeed."

He swam off, and soon came back with a beautiful horse, whose white mane streamed like foam in the water.

"I never knew that the white waves I saw rolling in to shore were really and truly the manes of horses!" said John in surprise.

The merman helped him up, and then sat on the horse behind him sideways, for his tail was rather awkward to manage on horseback.

"Goodbye!" called John, waving to Sylfai and Pinkity.

The white horse rose to the surface of the water and then, with its foamy mane just showing above the waves, began to gallop along swiftly.

Poor Ella had suddenly missed

John, and was dreadfully worried about him. She was walking up and down by the sea, calling him. A host of little fish put their heads above the water and told her not to worry, but of course she couldn't understand a word they said. She wasn't under a sea-spell, like John.

The white horse rushed out on the beach, and John jumped off. Before he could call goodbye and thank the merman, the horse

had turned, and vanished once more. John went to look for Ella.

There she was, way along the beach, calling at the top of her voice: "John, John, where are you?"

"Here I am!" called John, and he raced up to her.

"Oh, John, where have you been?" asked Ella. "I have been so worried about you."

"I've been to the bottom of the sea to look for your ring," said John.

"And do you know, the Silver Merman had bought it for Pinkity! They wanted me to take it to you, but I said I knew you would much rather Pinkity had it, and I made them keep it."

"What are you talking about?" said Ella.

"Don't tell stories, John! Nobody can go to the bottom of the sea, except divers."

"But I did go!" said John sticking his hands into his pockets, as he always did when he was cross.

"Well, I don't believe you," said Ella. "You've just been hiding somewhere to give me a fright."

"I haven't," said John – and then a strange look came over his face. He had felt something peculiar at the bottom of one of his pockets. He pulled it out – and dear me – there was the ring!

"Goodness!" he said, in astonishment. "The merman must have slipped it into my pocket when I was in front of him on the white horse!

Look Ella!
Here's your ring – now
I expect you'll believe
me, won't you!"
Ella took the ring
with a cry of
delight, and slipped
it on her finger.
"I shall have to
believe you!" she said.
"You really are a dear
to find it for me!"

Then off they went together, and John spent the rest of the day telling Ella all about his exciting adventures with his new friends under the sea.